RYDER THE BITER

by Brandi
Barnett

Ryder the Biter By Brandi Barnett

Published By Isabella Media Inc 270 Bellevue Ave #1002,

Newport Ri 02840

www.isabellamedia.com

© 2018 Isabella Media Inc

iSBN-13: 978-1733041690

For permissions contact: requests@isabellamedia.com

This Book is dedicated to all the Ryder's out there. This is a book for us, written by us and for our students. Thank you to every educator that has helped me be successful as an elementary school counselor. Shout-out to all the administrators, the school nurses, the librarians, the secretaries, the office managers, the school psychologists, the speech pathologists, the occupational therapists, the janitors, the cafeteria workers, the paraprofessionals, the special education team, and the school counselors!

Special thank you: For my family, who have been supportive of this dream as i sat on this idea for over two years. To my niece, Malia you are one cool kid who inspired the development of this character! xoxo

Brandi Barnett

Hi, my name is Ryder! They say I like to bite

THEY CALL ME A BITER YOU SEE!

i GUESS iT'S BETTER THAN BEING A FIGHTER.

MY DAD IS ALWAYS SIGHING "OHHHHHHHHHHH"

MY MOM IS ALWAYS SHOUTING "NNNNOOOOOO"

BUT I AM RYDER AND I SAY "SOOOOOOOOOOOOOOO"

"TEETH ARE NOT FOR BITING,"

SO THEY'VE SAID.

BUT i AM NOT SURE THEY KNOW

i DON'T LiKE iT ANYWAY!

if THEY'RE NOT FOR BiTING THEN WHAT ARE THEY FOR?

HAVE YOU EVER TRiED TO EAT WITHOUT ALL OF YOURS?

THE DENTIST SAYS I HAVE SO MANY TEETH.

THERE ARE 20 I BELIEVE.

HE SHOWS ME HOW TO COUNT THEM.

HE SAID, "THERE ARE MORE THAN YOU CAN SEE."

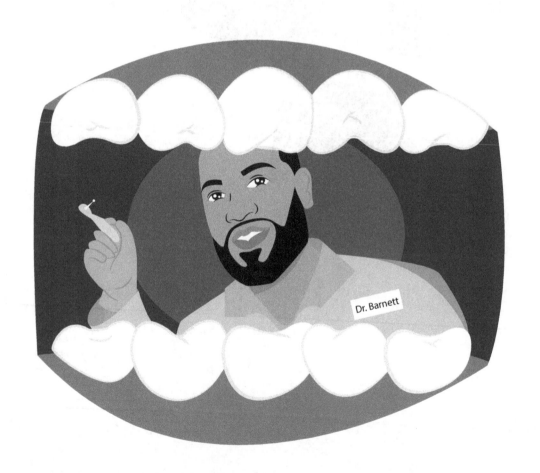

But there is this one kid in the class i do not like

His name was, oh it doesn't matter!

HE SAT IN MY SEAT. HE PULLED MY HAIR.

HE TOLD ME SPIDERMAN WASN'T FOR GIRLS.

THERE ARE PLAY CENTERS IN CLASS WITH MS. LYNN YOU SEE!
I HAD BEEN PATIENTLY WAITING SINCE YESTERDAY AT THREE.
IT'S THE FINAL BIG ACTIVITY OF THE DAY.
BEFORE SHE TOLD US TO PACK-UP FOR THE DAY.

"IT'S CENTERS," SHE EXCLAIMS!

—⁓—

I RAN TO MINE. THERE'S NO SHAME IN MY GAME.

"iTS COMPUTER TiME," SHE SHOUTS TO A GROUP.
i HAVE THE BLOCKS, BUT iT'S TiME TO MOVE.
i RUSHED AND PUT AWAY MY BLOCKS YOU SEE
iT'S NO LONGER MY TURN, i MOVED ON YOU SEE!

THAT WHAT-IS-HIS-NAME GETS IN MY WAY
I'M NOT HAPPY. "PLEASE MOVE" I START TO COMPLAIN.
HE POINTED TO THE PRETEND CENTER WITH MY NAME
I SCREAMED AND YELLED....NOOOOOOOOOOOO LET ME EXPLAIN!

i CRiED. i YELLED. i SCREAMED AND SHOUTED.

i OPENED MY MOUTH BUT NO WORDS CAME OUT.

i SAW HiM PLAYiNG AND LAUGHiNG AT ME.
SHE CALMLY TOLD ME iT'S TiME FOR ME TO.....

"EYES CLOSED,

BREATHE THROUGH YOUR NOSE,

HANDS ON YOUR BELLY, NOW LET'S GO

IN THROUGH YOUR SNOUT

AND OUT THROUGH YOUR MOUTH"

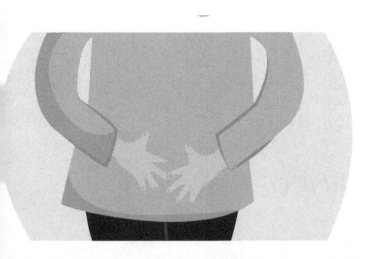

3 2 1 BLOW

1 2 3 LET'S GO" WE SAID.

SHE WALKED AWAY TO LET ME TRY!

SHE TRIED TO HELP

WE BOTH SIGHED!

i DiDN'T WANT iT.

So i CRiED. i YELLED. i SCREAMED AND SHOUTED.

i OPENED MY MOUTH BUT NOTHiNG CAME OUT.

MS. LYNN ASKED ME "WHAT IS THE FUSS ALL ABOUT"

BUT I WAS MAD SO I SAT AND POUTED.

SHE CALMLY TOLD ME

"IT'S NOT YOUR CENTER, SWEET BABY"

⁓

I SHRUGGED AND TURNED AND SAID

"WELL MAYBE!"

HE LAUGHED. i CRIED. HE SMILED. i FROWNED.

AND BEFORE YOU KNEW iT...i TOOK A BiTE OUT OF CRIME!

HE YELLED "SHE BiT."

YEP! i DiD!

WHATEVER HiS NAME CRied TO THE TEACHER.

i CRied LOUDER. i POiNTED. HE POiNTED. WHOSE FAULT

NOT MiNE EiTHER.

i BLAMED SHEiLA, SHE'S JUST AS MEAN TOO!

iM SUPPOSED TO APOLOGiZE BUT i CAN'T.

i CRiED. i YELLED. i SCREAMED AND SHOUTED.

i OPENED MY MOUTH BUT NOTHiNG CAME OUT.

MY TEACHER ASKED ME "WHAT WAS THE FUSS ALL ABOUT"

BUT i WAS SO MAD SO i SAT AND POUTED.

SHE GENTLY TAPPED MY CHAIR
AS A REMINDER
"EYES CLOSED,
BREATHE THROUGH YOUR NOSE,
HANDS ON YOUR BELLY, NOW LET'S GO
IN THROUGH YOUR SNOUT
AND OUT THROUGH YOUR MOUTH
3 2 1 BLOW
1 2 3 LET'S GO" I SAID.

"YOUR HAT IS VERY MAGICAL" SHE SAID

WAIT! WHAT! "OH THANK YOU" I REPLIED.

I NO LONGER FELT MAD. I WAS NOT SAD.

I FELT WARM AND BUBBLY. I WAS GLAD.

MS. LYNN HAD THIS MAGICAL SUPERHERO POWER.

SHE KISSED BOO-BOOS, HUGGED AWAY CRIES

SHE SMILED AT ALL OF US AND MISSED US WHEN WE WERE DOWN.

SHE WAS OUR CLASSROOM SUPERHERO.

ONE DAY, I WOULD LIKE TO BE HER!

My teacher walked me to the safe place.

it's just her and i. me and her.

CRAYONS. PAINTS. WATER. BRUSHES.

THE COLD PAINT FELT GOOD ON MY HOT HANDS.

IT MADE MY TOES WIGGLE AND I WANTED TO DO A HAPPY DANCE.

IT MADE ME SMILE.

NO LONGER A FROWN.

NO MORE YELLING

NO MORE LAYING ON THE GROUND.

i HUGGED MS.lynn FOR ONE lAST TiME.

"SORRY" i SAiD TO MY FRiENDS iN liNE.

MY YElliNG HURT THEiR liSTENiNG EARS

iT WASN'T VERY NiCE.

SHE GAVE ME A WINK

PATTED FOR ME TO COME SIT IN THE LEADER CHAIR.

I THINK SHE HAS SOMETHING TO SHARE.

IT'S THE CLASS SOCK PUPPET "MR BEAR".

WE CALLED HIM "MR. BEAR" ALTHOUGH HE WAS A DUCK!

"RYDER, USE YOUR WORDS" SHE REMINDED ME, GENTLY.

AS NICOLE ASKED ME TO SHARE MR. BEAR.

THIS TIME I WANTED TO HIT, KICK AND NOT SHARE.

"I'M SCARED" NICOLE WAS IN FOR A SCARE.

i THREW BLOCKS
i THREW THE SOCK.
i KiCKED SUSiE.
i'D JUST LOSE iT!

"NICE HANDS," SHE OFFERS TO REMIND ME.

SHE EVEN HELPS ME TO BELLY BREATHE.

HER GENTLE CALM VOICE SOOTHES ME

AS I HEAR HER SAY:

"EYES CLOSED,

BREATHE THROUGH YOUR NOSE,

HANDS ON YOUR BELLY, NOW LET'S GO

IN THROUGH YOUR SNOUT

AND OUT THROUGH YOUR MOUTH

3 2 1 BLOW

1 2 3 LET'S GO" I SAID.

I DIDN'T CRY. I DIDN'T YELL.

I DIDN'T EVEN SCREAM OR SHOUT.

I OPENED MY MOUTH AND MY WORDS CAME OUT!

MY TEACHER THIS TIME DIDN'T HAVE TO ASK ME

WHAT THE FUSS WAS ABOUT...

BECAUSE LAST NIGHT I'VE LEARNED

WHEN I CRIED.

I YELLED.

I SCREAMED AND SHOUTED.

MY MOM DIDN'T ASK ME, "WHAT WAS THE FUSS ALL ABOUT".

SHE GAVE ME TIME-OUT.

i've learned when i get mad or sad

i wiggle and tingle.

when you do the crying, then you have to do the time!

"EYES CLOSED,

BREATHE THROUGH YOUR NOSE,

HANDS ON YOUR BELLY, NOW LET'S GO

IN THROUGH YOUR SNOUT

AND OUT THROUGH YOUR MOUTH"

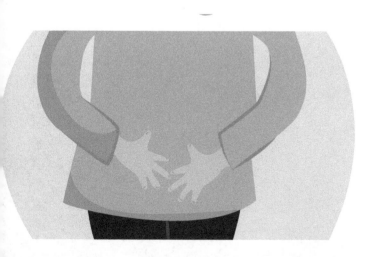

3 2 1 BLOW

1 2 3 LET'S GO" WE SAID.

CPSIA information can be obtained
at www.ICGtesting.com
Printed in the USA
JSHW021033310121
11286JS00005BA/64

9 781733 041690